For Vivienne Flesher,
with growing affection.
— W. S.

Book design by
Paul Donald | Graphic Detail.
Typeset in Monotype Walbaum
and Base Nine.

The illustrations
in this book were rendered
in Adobe Photoshop.

Printed in Hong Kong.

0-8118-2689-9

Library of Congress
Cataloging-in-Publication Data
Schumaker, Ward.
In my garden : a counting book;
by Ward Schumaker.
p. cm.

Summary:
In this garden the reader
learns to count from one
watering can to ten snails,
from twenty weepy onions
to fifty cherries and even
to 233 peas.

ISBN 0-8118-2689-9
[1. Gardens-Fiction.
2. Counting.]
I. Title.
PZ7.S3925 In 2000
[E]--dc21

99-006880

Distributed in Canada
by RAINCOAST BOOKS
8680 Cambie Street
Vancouver, British Columbia
V6P 6M9

10 9 8 7 6 5 4 3 2 1

CHRONICLE BOOKS
85 Second Street
San Francisco, California 94105

www.chroniclebooks.com/Kids

In My Garden

A COUNTING BOOK

BY WARD SCHUMAKER

chronicle books · san francisco

In my garden,
I have **1** one
watering
can

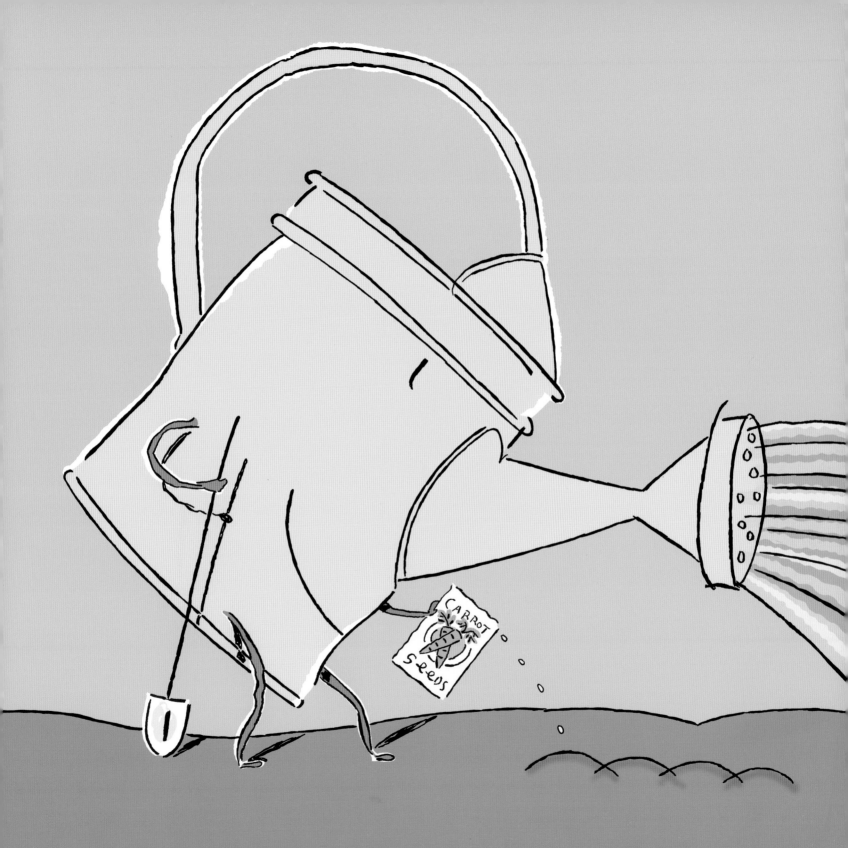

Two pots 2
for planting

Three **3** flowers dancing

Four
shady
trees...

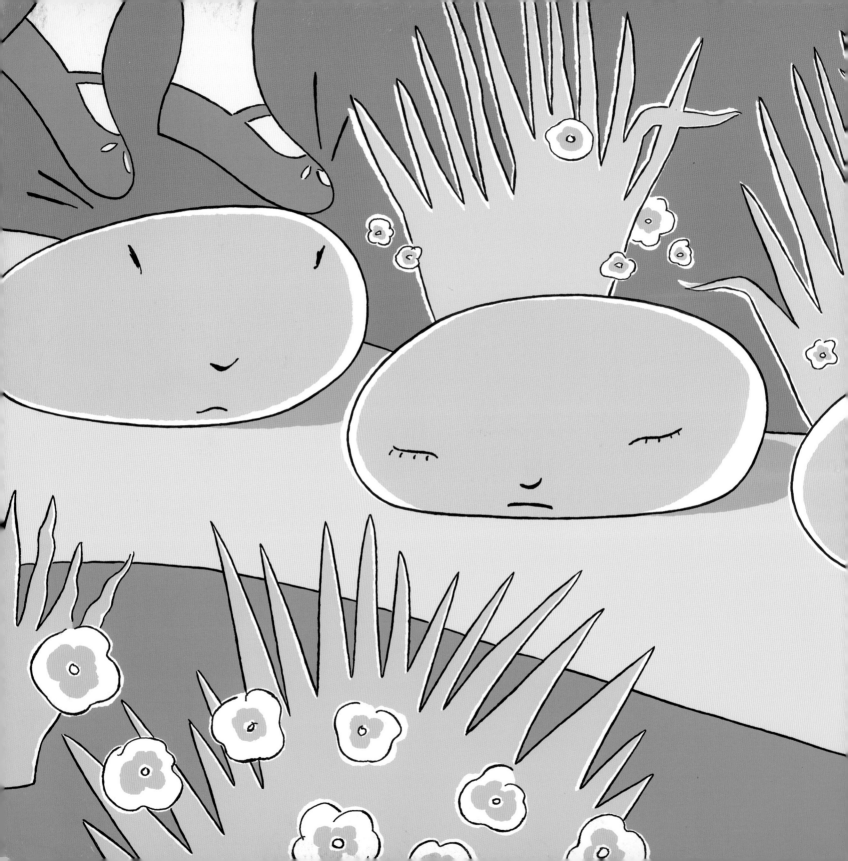

and five stones
for stepping.

5

There are

6

six
fat worms

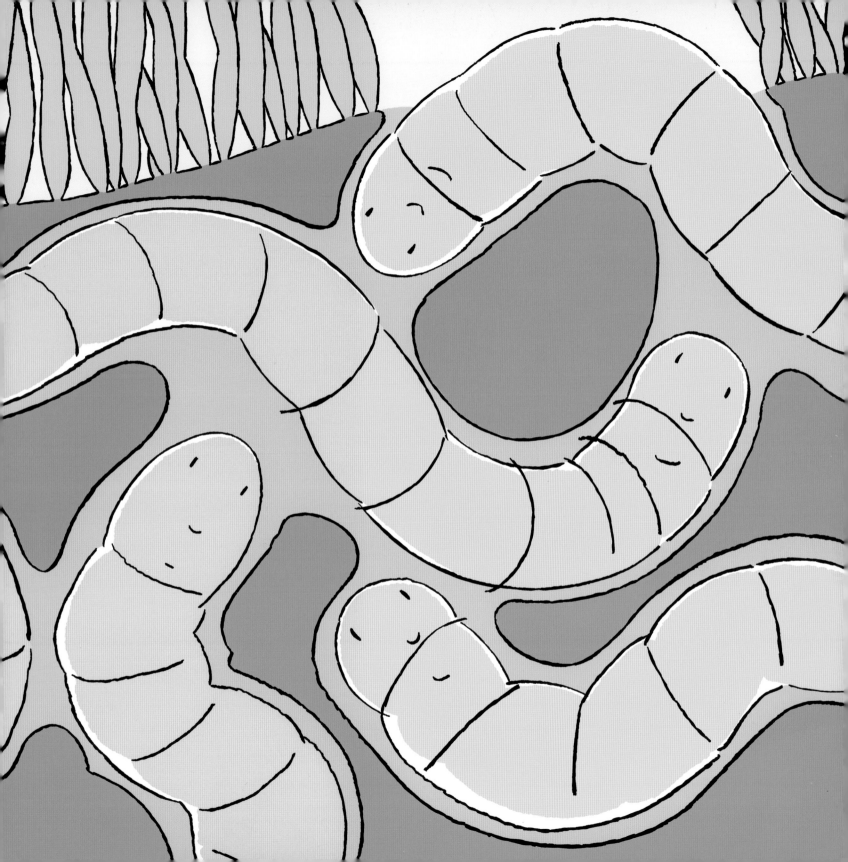

Seven 7
singing birds

8 Eight bees a-buzzing

9
Nine butterflies...

And **10** ten snails
late for dinner.

In my garden,
I grow

20

twenty weeping
onions

30 Thirty
purple grapes

Forty
crabby
apples

Fifty **50** cherries
for pies
I'll bake...

And

233

two-hundred
thirty-three
plump little peas!

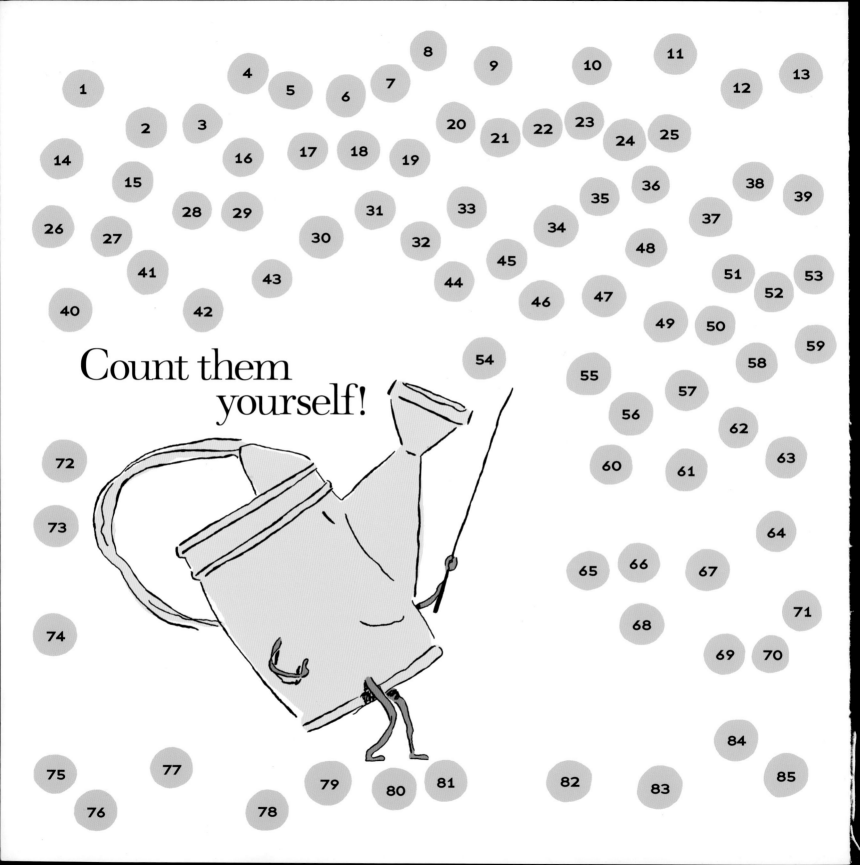

Count them
yourself!

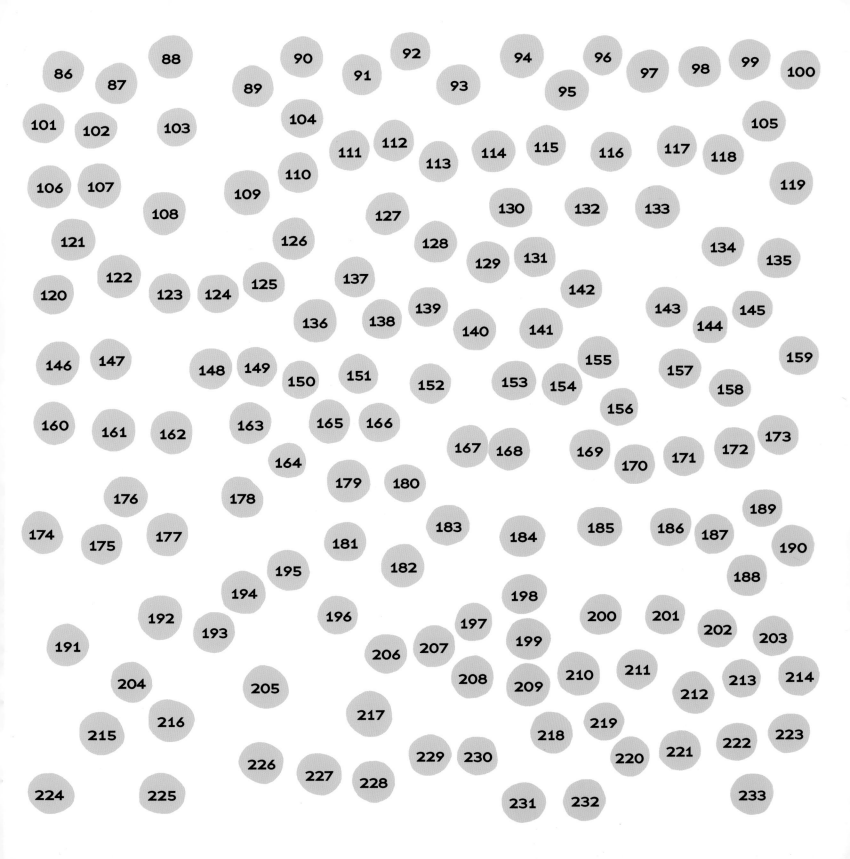

In my garden,
there are so many things
I can count on
to make me happy!

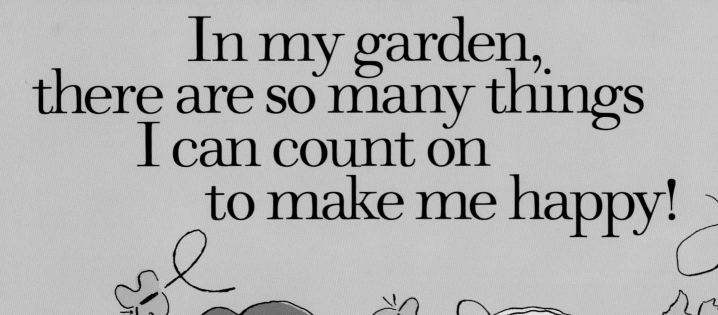

Bathtime
PiggyWiggy

Christyan and Diane Fox

Handprint Books 🖐 Brooklyn, New York